Jack Takes the CAKE

by Marni McGee

illustrated by Dana Regan

Troll

Once, a long time ago, there was a
boy whose name was Jack.

Jack and his puppy went to see his
grandmother almost every day.
And almost every day, she gave him
something to take home to his papa.

One day Granny gave Jack a slice
of cake.

"Papa loves cake," said Jack.

"Yes," said Granny. "Always has.
Always will. Take him this cake.
Tell him it came from me."

"Yes," said Jack. "I will."

"You are a good boy, Jack," said Granny. She kissed the freckles on his face and sent him on his way.

Jack took the cake in his hand. He held it very tight. By the time he got home, there was nothing left but a fist full of crumbs.

His papa asked, "What do you have there, Jack?"

"Cake," said Jack, "from Granny."

"Cake?" cried Papa. "Jack, you must have pudding where your brains should be! That is no way to carry cake. But do not worry, Jack. I will tell you how to do it. You put that cake in a napkin. You set the napkin in your cap. You put the cap on your head, and then you come on home."

"Oh," said Jack. "I see. Now, Papa, here is your cake."

Papa made a face. "I am not a bird, my boy. I do not like crumbs."

So Jack ate the crumbs himself. They tasted very good.

The next day Jack and his puppy
went to see his granny again. This
time she gave him some fine, fresh
butter.

Granny said, "Your papa loves butter.
Always has. Always will. Take it
home to your papa. Tell him it came
from me."

"Yes," said Jack. "I will."

"You are a good boy, Jack," said
Granny. She kissed the freckles on
his face and sent him on his way.

Jack did not forget what his papa had told him. He put a napkin around the butter. He set the napkin in his cap and put it on his head.

But it was a hot day—a *very* hot day.
Soon the butter began to melt. It
melted, and then it melted some more.
By the time Jack got home, he had
butter in his hair and on his freckles.
He had butter down his neck and
on his arms. He even had butter in
his ears!

"Jack," said Papa. "What happened
to you?"

"Butter," said Jack. "Butter happened
to me. Granny sent it home for you."

16

"Jack," cried Papa, "you must have pudding where your brains should be! That is no way to carry butter. But do not worry, Jack. I will tell you how to do it. Every now and then you must stop beside the creek. You must dip that butter in the water. You cool it, and then you cool it some more."

"Oh," said Jack. "I see. Do you want your butter now?"

Papa made a face. "I am not a cat, my boy. I will not lick butter from your head. You must wash it off."

"Yes," said Jack. "I will."

He jumped into a tub of warm water.
He poured water on his head. He
poured it on his neck and arms. He
poured it on all of his freckles. That
water felt good!

Jack grinned.

The next day Jack went to see his
granny once again.

This time she gave him a loaf of
fresh, warm bread.

"Papa loves bread," said Jack.

"Yes," said Granny. "Always has. Always will. Take him this bread. Tell him it came from me."

"Yes," said Jack. "I will."

"You are a good boy, Jack," said Granny. She kissed the freckles on his face and sent him on his way.

Jack did not forget what Papa had said. On the way home, he stopped every now and then. He dipped the bread in the cool water of the creek.

By the time he got home, that loaf
of bread was all wet!

"What do you have there, Jack?"
asked Papa.

"Bread," said Jack, "from Granny. She made it fresh for you."

"Bread?" cried Papa. "You dipped bread in the creek, Jack? You *do* have pudding where your brains should be! That is no way to carry bread. But I will not tell you how to do it. I will not tell you how to do anything! Not anymore! I will go see Granny myself."

Jack was sad.

His puppy jumped up to lick
his hand.

Papa said, "I made a berry pie. It is a good pie, Jack. I do not want you to squeeze it in your fist. I do not want you to put it in your cap or cool it in the creek. You hear me now, Jack?"

"Yes, Papa," said Jack. "I will not do those things."

Papa smiled. "You are a good boy, Jack—with pudding where your brains should be."

Papa walked out the door, and off he went to see Granny.

Jack took the puppy in his arms.

"Puppy," said Jack. "Do you see that
berry pie my papa made?
I will not squeeze it in my fist.
I will not put it in my cap.
I will not dip it in the creek.

"I know what to do with pie. No one needs to tell me. I do not have pudding in my head where all my brains should be!"

And then Jack and his puppy ate
that pie.
Every single slice.
Every single bite!

Jack grinned. "The way to carry pie
is in your tummy. That is where a
good berry pie should be!"